For Fred Ehrlich, who insisted
I go with him to First Night Boston,
on December 31, 1996—HZ

Text copyright © 1999 by Harriet Ziefert. Illustrations copyright © 1999 by S. D. Schindler.
All rights reserved. This book, or parts thereof, may not be reproduced in any form without permission
in writing from the publisher. G. P. Putnam's Sons, a division of Penguin Putnam Books for Young Readers,
345 Hudson Street, New York, NY 10014. G. P. Putnam's Sons, Reg. U.S. Pat & Tm. Off.
Published simultaneously in Canada. Printed in Hong Kong. Text set in Meridien Bold. Designed by Patrick Collins.
The art for this book was created using colored pencils and magic markers on midnight blue pastel paper.

Library of Congress Catalog-in-Publication Data. Ziefert, Harriet. First night / by Harriet Ziefert; illustrated by S. D. Schindler. p. cm.
Summary: Although others participate by driving, riding, and making music, Amanda Dade leads the parade to welcome the arrival
of the new year. ISBN 0-399-23120-X [I. Parades—Fiction. 2. New Year—Fiction. 3. Stories in rhyme.] I. Schindler, S. D., ill. II. Title.
PZ8.3.Z47Fi 1999 [E]—dc21 98-48999 CIP AC 10 9 8 7 6 5 4 3 2 1 First Impression

FIRST NIGHT

by **Harriet Ziefert**

illustrated by **S. D. Schindler**

G. P. Putnam's Sons • New York

Amanda Dade
led the parade.

Officer Dowd
cleared the crowd,

but Amanda Dade
led the parade.

Mayor McSnorse
rode a horse.

Mayor McSnorse
rode a horse.
Officer Dowd
cleared the crowd,
but Amanda Dade
led the parade.

**Fire Chief Stumper
drove the pumper.**

Fire Chief Stumper
drove the pumper.
Mayor McSnorse
rode a horse.
Officer Dowd
cleared the crowd,
but Amanda Dade
led the parade.

Reginald Crumpet
played the trumpet.

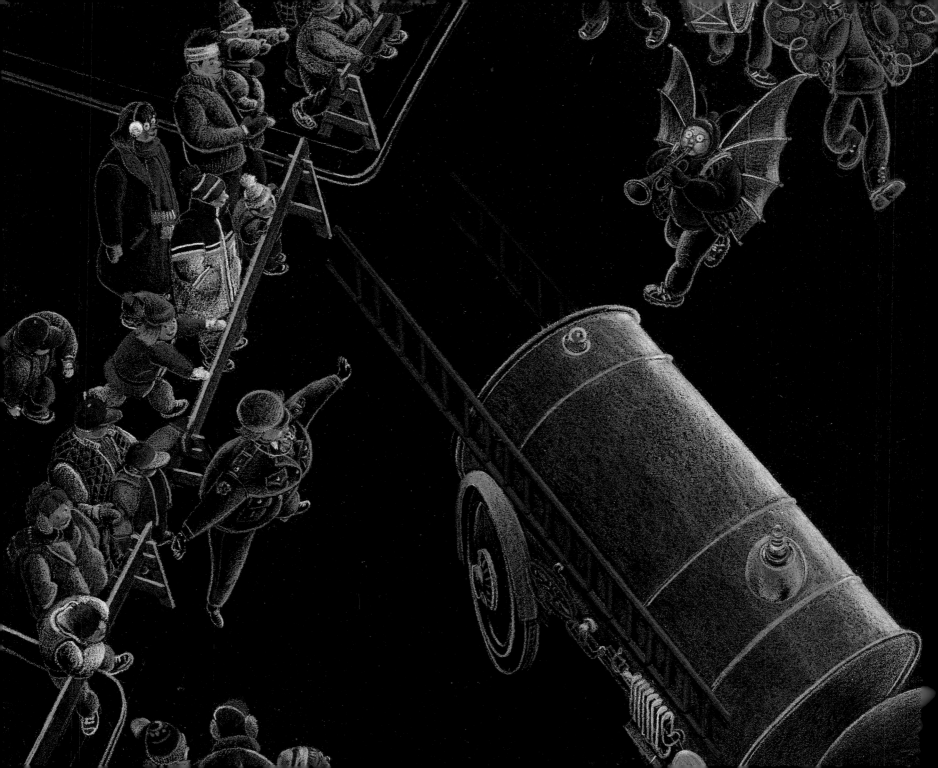

Reginald Crumpet
played the trumpet.
Fire Chief Stumper
drove the pumper.
Mayor McSnorse
rode a horse.
Officer Dowd
cleared the crowd,
but Amanda Dade
led the parade.

Grandma Hooter
rode a scooter.

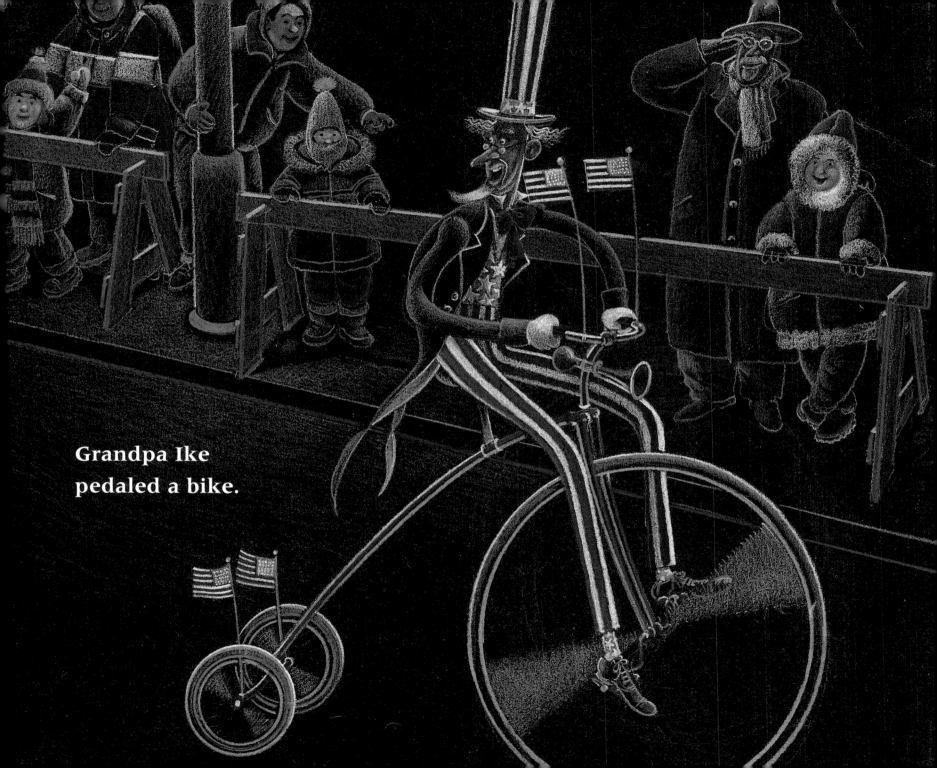

Grandpa Ike
pedaled a bike.

Grandma Hooter rode a scooter.
Grandpa Ike pedaled a bike.
Reginald Crumpet
played the trumpet.
Fire Chief Stumper
drove the pumper.
Mayor McSnorse
rode a horse.
Officer Dowd
cleared the crowd,
but Amanda Dade
led the parade.

Captain Byron
blew the siren.

Captain Byron
blew the siren,
but Amanda Dade
stopped the parade.

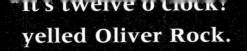

"It's twelve o'clock!"
yelled Oliver Rock.

HAPPY NEW YEAR!